TREES ARE FOREVER

Written by:
Hugh C. Griffin

Illustrated by:
Margaret Wilkins

Edited by:
Mary Ann Griffin

To order additional copies of this book, contact:
Xlibris
1-888-795-4274
www.Xlibris.com
Orders@Xlibris.com

ISBN: Softcover   978-1-4363-4854-6
        Hardcover   978-1-4363-4855-3

Library of Congress Control Number: 2008905051

Print information available on the last page

Rev. date: 02/22/2020

For

Clare, Molly, Matthew,
Gordon, Maeve, Aidan
and trees everywhere.

High on a mountain there were many trees. There was a large Oak tree, a Maple tree, a Birch tree, a Cedar tree, an Elm tree, an Ash tree, a Pine tree,

a Redwood,
a Hickory tree,
and a Walnut tree.

They all got along
and lived happily
on the mountain
for many years.

One day, they heard
a loud noise.
"What is that?"
said the Oak tree.

"It sounds like a tractor,"
said the Maple tree.

"Oh no!
It is a tractor... headed our way,"
said the Pine tree. "We're all going
to be cut down," screamed the Ash tree.

"Right," said the Ash tree. "And maybe if we wish real hard about what we want to be in our next life, our wish will come true!"

...And he was made into a beautiful rocking chair that sat on a shaded porch where he enjoyed the fresh air and sunsets with his owner.

...And she was made into a strong
sailboat
that traveled
all around the world,
and she saw all the far away places
she had heard so much about!

The Hickory tree said,"I want to do something that really helps people."

...And he was made into beautiful walking canes that helped many people get around and enjoy life.

The Elm tree said,

"I want to make music in my next life."

...And he was carved into beautiful violins that were played to create magical music!

The Sugar Pine said, "I want to be around children; I love little children!"

...And he was made into a beautiful carousel horse on which happy children rode every day!

The Cedar tree said, "I want a nice family life."

...And he was made into a beautiful house where a mother and a father and two children lived and even had a house for their dog!

...And he was made into school desks and chairs at which children learned to read and write.

And the Birch tree said, "I love having friendly birds sit on my branches. I want to still be with them."

Margaret Watkins

And he was carved into beautiful bird houses, and all his bird friends came to live with him!

...And he was made into a baseball bat, a hockey stick, a basketball backboard, a football goal post, and a jumping fence for riders!

...And he was made into a footbridge that crossed a stream so that children and their families could enjoy nature walks in a newly planted forest!

Trees Are Forever!

And this Tree book was printed on re-cycled paper From Trees.

Hugh Griffin is an avid horseman, sailor and
practicing appellate lawyer. He lives in Chicago
with his wife of 42 years, Mary Ann.

Ms. Margaret Wilkins has written, illustrated, and published her first children's book
"Life's Little Inspirations ©", in 2008, available through Xlibris. Margaret loves to
travel the world, then return to her schipperke, Belle Luna, in sweet home Chicago.
She is also a certified volunteer Tree Keeper #860, a group dedicated to developing
and maintaining our "urban forests" and bringing national care and awareness to our
wonderful friends, The Trees! Feel free to join us at www.openlands.org.

Printed in the United States
By Bookmasters